Secret Kingdom

WITHDRAWN

D0967741

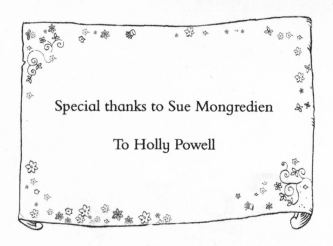

Special thanks to Sue Mongredien

To Holly Powell

ORCHARD BOOKS

First published in Great Britain in 2013 by Orchard Books
This edition published in 2017 by The Watts Publishing Group

5 7 9 10 8 6 4

© 2013 Hothouse Fiction Limited
Illustrations © Orchard Books 2013

A CIP catalogue record for this book is available from the British Library.

ISBN 978 1 40832 339 7

Printed in Great Britain by Clays Ltd, St Ives plc

MIX
Paper from
responsible sources
FSC® C104740

The paper and board used in this book are made from wood from responsible sources

Orchard Books
An imprint of Hachette Children's Group
Part of The Watts Publishing Group Limited
Carmelite House, 50 Victoria Embankment, London EC4Y 0DZ

An Hachette UK Company
www.hachette.co.uk
www.hachettechildrens.co.uk

Series created by Hothouse Fiction
www.hothousefiction.com

Swan Palace

ROSIE BANKS

ORCHARD

This is the
Secret Kingdom

Swan Palace

Contents

A New
Adventure

"Just wait till I get my hands on you,"
sneered the evil enchanter in a bone-
chilling voice. His eyes glinted as he held
up a spellbook. "You'll be sorry you
crossed me. Now come here!"

Summer Hammond let out a squeak
of fright and hid her face in a pillow.

She and her two best friends, Ellie and Jasmine, were curled up on her bed watching a film together, and it was getting *very* scary! The characters in the film, Lauren and Sam, were trying to escape from a horrible wizard, and Summer couldn't bear to watch him chase them. She clutched her pillow as the enchanter gave a horrible gloating cackle. "What's happening?" she asked in a muffled voice.

Ellie giggled. "Summer! You're not really scared, are you? This is the most exciting bit!"

"Mwah-ha-ha!" cried Jasmine, copying the enchanter's cackle as she tossed her long black hair. "You'll be sorry you crossed me. Now come here!"

Summer squealed as first Jasmine

and then Ellie began tickling her. The pillow fell off her head and she laughed helplessly. "Stop! Stop!" she shouted, feeling weak and breathless. "Help!"

Suddenly, all three of them toppled off the bed together with a bump and lay in a tangle on Summer's floor, still laughing.

"That baddie doesn't seem so scary any more," Summer giggled, struggling to a sitting position.

"Look – Lauren and Sam have escaped anyway," Ellie said, pointing at the screen. "Just like we got away from the giant in Wildflower Wood."

The girls fell silent for a moment, remembering their last exciting adventure in the Secret Kingdom. Ever since they'd found a mysterious Magic Box at their school fair, the girls had been special friends of the magical land, helping King Merry and his loyal subjects outwit his horrible sister Queen Malice, and protecting the elves, brownies and other wonderful creatures living there.

The last time the girls had been whisked away to the Secret Kingdom,

they'd discovered that Queen Malice was
up to her trouble-causing ways again.
Using her evil magic, Malice had cast
a spell to unleash all the baddies from
Summer's book of fairytales and sent
them into the kingdom to cause chaos.
The girls had helped stop an enormous
giant from destroying Wildflower Wood,
but they knew there were still five other
villains somewhere out there.

Jasmine glanced over at the Magic
Box, up on Summer's chest of drawers.
It was a wooden box with an oval
mirror set into its lid, surrounded by
six gleaming green gems. The sides of
the box were decorated with beautiful
carvings of mermaids, unicorns and other
magical creatures, and inside was a
collection of the special gifts the girls had

been given during their adventures.

Jasmine went to pick up the box, then sat down on Summer's bed with it in her lap. "I wonder what's been happening in the Secret Kingdom since we were there," she said, gently running her fingers over the carvings. "I've been trying to work out who the other fairytale baddies might be. We saw a wolf, didn't we? That must be the Big Bad Wolf."

Summer shivered, even though the

room was warm. "I love animals but
I still wouldn't like to meet a big bad
wolf," she said, twisting her blonde
pigtail round her fingers. "Think how
frightened all the little brownies would
be, too!"

"What if one of the baddies is an evil
enchanter, like the one in the film just
now?" Ellie added. "I wouldn't want to
meet *him* either."

Jasmine gasped. "I think we're about
to find out what *is* going on in the Secret
Kingdom," she said, pointing at the box.
"Look!"

Summer, Ellie and Jasmine all stared
excitedly at the wooden box. Something
magical was happening! The mirror on
top gleamed with a silvery light, then
sparks rippled across it.

"It's a message from Trixi," Summer breathed as loopy handwriting appeared on the mirror, word by word. Trixi was the pretty royal pixie who helped King Merry in the Secret Kingdom. The girls crowded eagerly round the box and read the message.

"My friends, we need help at the double.
A nasty villain is causing trouble.
Come to the palace gleaming white
Where you may see our birds in flight."

"A nasty villain," Jasmine repeated, feeling her skin prickle at the thought of another adventure.

"Hmm," said Summer with a little frown. "A palace gleaming white? King Merry's Enchanted Palace is pink – that can't be the answer."

Ellie thought back over all their adventures, trying to work out what the riddle could mean. "I don't remember seeing a white palace," she said slowly, "but we have seen white birds. Do you remember the swans?"

"Oh, yes!" Jasmine cried. "Riding the swans was amazing." She would never forget how they had tumbled into the Secret Kingdom that first exciting time, each landing on the back of one of King Merry's royal swans. The graceful white birds had taken them soaring through the sky, with the whole of the Secret Kingdom laid out like a green and blue map below, twinkling with magic here and there.

"The swans were lovely," Summer

agreed, remembering how soft their big white feathers had felt, and how their beaks had glittered as if they'd been dipped in golden paint. "But we still don't know the answer to the riddle."

Just then, the lid of the box gave a soft creak and opened. A small square of faded parchment lay inside and Ellie took it out at once, opening it to reveal a map of the Secret Kingdom. "I bet the answer to the riddle is somewhere on here," she said.

The map wasn't an ordinary map – it was like a magical window down onto the kingdom. The girls pored over it, smiling as they recognised places they'd visited. Bubbles spilled out of the top of Bubble Volcano, where they had met the adorable bubblebees. A pair of young

unicorns, their horns gleaming silver,
pranced in Unicorn Valley, their sparkly
tails swishing behind them. A dream
dragon flew gently over Dream Dale,
and as Jasmine leaned in to take a closer
look at the picture of mermaids diving
in Mermaid Reef, she was sure she could
hear the rushing of the waves.

But Summer's eye had been caught
by a tiny flock of birds drifting across
the map. "Swan
Palace," she
read aloud,
pointing at
an elegant
white
building beside
an azure lake.
"That must be it!"

The Swan Queen

Summer, Jasmine and Ellie put their hands on the Magic Box. "The answer is…Swan Palace!" they chorused.

A bright silver light poured from the box, glittering with magic. Ellie blinked at the dazzling sparkles, then noticed a familiar figure twirling through the air on a leaf. "Trixi!" she exclaimed happily.

Trixi beamed and
waved. Today she
was wearing a
striped hat on
her tumbling
blonde hair,
and a frilly
skirt made out
of pink flower
petals. She darted
up, kissing each girl's
nose in turn. "Hello, there," she said.
"I'm so glad you got my message."

"Is everything all right, Trixi?" Summer
asked in concern.

Trixi's blue eyes clouded over. "There's
a problem at Swan Palace – I'm worried
it's another fairytale baddie," she said.
"King Merry's already gone there to

help, but…" She lowered her voice, glancing over her shoulder as if she didn't want to be heard. "Well, knowing His Highness, he might be making things worse," she said with a wink.

Jasmine smiled. King Merry was kind and jolly, but most of his ideas and inventions went wrong. Even his best invention, the Magic Box, had been made accidentally! "Can we help?" she asked hopefully. The three friends knew that time in their world would stand still when they were in the Secret Kingdom, so nobody would even know they'd gone.

"Yes, please," Trixi replied. "That would be wonderful. Hold hands then, girls, and we'll be off!"

Ellie, Jasmine and Summer quickly held

hands so that they were standing in a circle. Trixi tapped her pixie ring against the Magic Box and chanted a rhyme:

"Brave helpers, now you must not fail,
Return these villains to their
fairytale."

Trixi's words flickered on the lid of the box for a few seconds, sparkling a bright silver, then the letters separated and rushed upwards, shimmering with light to form a glittering whirlwind above the girls' heads.

Jasmine, Summer and Ellie clung to one another as they were whisked up and away from Summer's bedroom in another dazzling flash of light. They were off to the Secret Kingdom again!

Moments later, their feet touched solid ground once more and the girls found themselves on the banks of a beautiful turquoise lake. The water rippled peacefully as the sun cast golden sparkles on its surface, with the occasional glint of orange fish swimming deep below. Large white swans sailed elegantly across

the lake, their necks curved proudly. Summer noticed that one swan seemed to be looking straight at them, and she gave her a friendly wave. This swan was slightly bigger than the others, with golden tips to her wings and an unusual tuft of feathers on her head.

"It's lovely here," Ellie sighed happily. "So lovely I can't believe anything bad

could possibly happen."

Trixi looked uneasy. "Let's hope you're right," she said. "Come on, I'll take you to the palace."

The girls followed Trixi through a small wood of evergreen trees. The air smelled fresh and clean, and two large yellow butterflies fluttered between the trees above the girls' heads.

Jasmine noticed that her friends were

now wearing pretty jewelled tiaras sparkling with jewels, and reached up to touch her own tiara, smiling. Whenever they went to the Secret Kingdom, their tiaras magically appeared on their heads to let everyone else know that they were Very Important Friends of the Kingdom.

They emerged from the woodland, and the girls all gasped. There before them was the palace: a large white building standing on stilts by the edge of the lake. It had carved towers shaped like swans at either side, and large arched windows. Sunlight twinkled against the white stone walls as if there was magic all around.

Trixi led the girls up a flight of steps towards a tall golden front door. Just as they reached it, the door opened and out burst King Merry, his purple robe

flapping behind him and his crown
wonky on his curly white hair. "Thank
goodness, thank goodness," he cried, his
spectacles slipping down his nose. "I'm
so glad you're here. The Swan Queen
urgently needs your help."

At that moment, one of the swans
on the lake flapped her great white

wings and rose out of the water, swooping across to the palace steps and landing beside the girls. It was the swan Summer had noticed before, she realised, recognising the tuft of feathers on her head. But something strange was happening. With a flurry of white magic sparkles, the swan began to transform before the girls' eyes!

Her body grew tall and slender. Her plumage became a long white dress, trimmed with feathers. Her wings turned to arms, and her webbed black feet became a pair of ordinary feet in silver ballet slippers. To the girls' astonishment, within just a few seconds, the swan had completely transformed into a beautiful woman wearing a silver crown on her head.

Ellie's mouth dropped open and
Summer stared in amazement. "Wow,"
Jasmine whispered.

Trixi gave a dainty curtsey. "Your
Majesty," she said respectfully.

Summer, Jasmine and Ellie dropped
into curtseys too. "Your Majesty," they
echoed in a chorus. It was the Swan
Queen herself!

The Second Baddie

The Swan Queen smiled at the three girls. Her skin was as white as the palace stone, but her eyes sparkled a clear blue, just like the lake.

"Hello," she said in a low, musical voice. "I see from your tiaras that you are the human girls I have heard so much about. You are very welcome here. I am delighted to meet you."

Ellie gulped. She was so in awe of the beautiful Swan Queen her knees felt wobbly. Even confident Jasmine looked a bit shy.

"It's lovely to meet you too," she said after a moment, dipping her head. "I'm Jasmine."

"I'm Ellie," said Ellie, recovering herself, "and this is Summer."

"Trixi said there had been some trouble here," Summer said politely. "If there's anything we can do to help, Your Majesty…?"

The Swan Queen smiled. "Thank you, my child," she said. "Let us proceed to the royal courtyard and I will explain the problem."

"Jolly good," King Merry said, looking relieved. He cast a fearful glance up to

the sky then followed the queen back
through the palace door. After a nod
from Trixi, Ellie, Summer and Jasmine
went inside too.

They found themselves in a spacious
entrance hall, which had an arched
white ceiling and a grand staircase that
swept up one side of the room. The floor
was speckled white marble, and the
queen's long dress billowed behind her as
she walked, making a soft swishing sound
on the stone.

The Swan Queen led them through
the hall and down a corridor, then into
a courtyard that was open to the blue
sky above. A fountain bubbled softly in
a central pool, and there were two trees
with scented white star-shaped flowers
at one end. In front of the trees stood an

ornate silver throne, trimmed with long white feathers.

The Swan Queen sat in the throne, then raised her arms up and sang a long, low note. The very air seemed to ripple with the sound, and the girls watched uncertainly.

"What's happening?" Summer whispered.

"She's calling the others," Trixi replied. "Just watch."

A moment later, the girls heard a distant rushing sound. Then, above their heads, a whole group of swans appeared flying in from the lake, their great wings flapping majestically. One by one the birds swooped to land in the courtyard – and as they did so, each transformed into a human dressed in simple white robes. They all had the same pale skin and blue eyes as the Swan Queen, and wore silver circlets on their heads.

"Good day, good day," said King Merry, smiling and waving at the swan-people. "Hello there, Silver. Hello, Snow! Nice to see you all again."

Once the last swan had landed and transformed, the Swan Queen addressed the crowd. "Thank you, everyone," she said. "Swans, let me introduce you to Summer, Ellie and Jasmine."

There was a ripple of noise as the swan-people recognised them and bent their heads politely.

"I have been the guardian of the skies here in the Secret Kingdom for many years," the Swan Queen explained. "King Merry and his royal ancestors trust me to wear the sky crown and keep the peace. With the help of my loyal swans, I ensure the safety of all who fly."

King Merry nodded. "It's true," he
told the girls. "The swans have done
a splendid job for as long as I can
remember." He bowed to the gathering
of swan-people. "The kingdom is
grateful to you all."

"Unfortunately," the Swan Queen
went on, "the skies have not been quite
so safe recently. We have had reports
from the mountain eagles and the forest
owls of a strange woman terrorising the
sky. She is said to dress in black and
wear a pointed hat. She doesn't fly with
wings like we birds. She rides on an
enchanted stick with bristles at one end."

"That sounds like a broomstick," Ellie
said, thinking aloud.

"She must be a witch!" Jasmine
exclaimed anxiously.

"What has she been doing?" Summer asked the queen nervously. She didn't like the sound of this witch at all.

"Terrible things," the Swan Queen replied, looking unhappy. "She uses bad magic to control the wind, whipping up strong storms which make flying a struggle. She knocks nests out of trees and breaks our precious eggs. She is a dangerous enemy, and we need to prepare for battle."

Just then, there came a loud, gloating cackle from above. It sounded very much like the enchanter's cackle from the film they'd been watching, Summer thought in alarm.

Everyone looked up to see a black shape flying overhead. The swan-people craned their necks back and made an unfriendly hissing sound.

Jasmine squinted to make out the shape high in the air. "It's a witch all right," she said, feeling shivery as she saw the pointy hat on the witch's head, and her flapping black cloak.

"There was a wicked witch in my book of fairytales," Summer remembered with despair. "She must be the second of the fairytale baddies!"

An Airborne Attack!

The Wicked Witch vanished from sight and a tense silence fell. "We'll do our best to send the witch back into the fairytale book," Ellie said bravely. "We managed it with the giant before."

The Swan Queen's expression was solemn. "Thank you," she replied. "The sooner we can make our skies safe again, the better."

"First of all, we need to track her down," Jasmine said thoughtfully. She gazed up at the sky, feeling helpless. How were she and her friends meant to chase after a witch who could fly away from them so quickly?

The Swan Queen seemed to read her mind. "We will be your wings," she declared. "Silver! Swoop! Longfeather! Please take these young ladies. Your Highness, allow me to transport you."

Three of the swan-people immediately pressed their hands together and touched them to their foreheads. White and silver magic sparkled around them as they transformed back into birds in an instant. The Swan Queen transformed too and beckoned King Merry to her with a graceful flick of her wingtip.

As he scrambled rather awkwardly onto her feathery back, the other three swans stepped towards the girls.

"Longfeather, at your service," said one in a jolly voice, allowing Jasmine to sit on his back.

"They call me Swoop," said the second, whose eyes were beady and bright.

"I'll ride with you, Swoop, if that's okay," Summer said politely, stroking his soft feathers as she clambered onto his back. "Thank you."

"And I'm Silver," said the third swan in a sweet, shy voice.

"Hello there," said Ellie, but she hesitated as she climbed onto the bird. "Um…Are we going to go *very* high?" she asked nervously. "It's just I'm a bit scared of heights."

"There's no need to worry," Silver replied, stretching out a wing to pat Ellie's arm comfortingly. "You'll be quite safe with me."

"You were fine when we flew with the dream dragons," Jasmine reminded her encouragingly. "And you can always shut your eyes."

"But then I won't see the witch, will I?" Ellie replied.

"Good idea – I might shut *my* eyes," Summer said, only half joking. She thought the witch sounded a bit scary.

"I'll ride with you, Ellie," Trixi said,
floating over on her leaf and settling
herself in Ellie's pocket. "Come on, let's
go."

The swans took off one after another –
first the Swan Queen, then Longfeather
with Jasmine and Swoop with Summer.
Then it was the turn of Ellie's swan,
Silver.

"Hold tight," she called as she spread
her strong wings wide. "Here we go!"

Ellie barely had time to feel scared as
the swan flapped her wings once, twice,
three times – and sailed up into the
air. She held tight to Silver, the wind
whipping her hair back from her face.
"Whoooaaa!" she gasped as the land
dropped away beneath her. She shut her

eyes quickly. "I can't look!"

"Oh, Ellie, you must," cried Jasmine. "It's amazing!"

"It's really fine," Summer added kindly. "Just open one eye and see!"

"You're quite safe," Trixi promised her. "It's fun!"

Ellie opened one eye a tiny crack and peered cautiously down, her heart

thudding. Below her was the lake, and further ahead she could see the purples and greens of the mountains, forests and meadows that made up the Secret Kingdom. She forgot all about being scared as she gazed at the incredible view. "Wow," she murmured, spotting the Enchanted Palace in the distance. "Everything looks so tiny!"

Silver caught up with Swoop and Longfeather and the three swans flew in a line together behind their queen. "It's so peaceful up here," Jasmine commented as they soared over a large forest. "I feel as if we're the only ones in the whole kingdom."

Longfeather looked anxious. "It's *too* quiet," he replied. "Normally the skies are filled with all the forest birds. They must be hiding from the witch today."

Summer hated imagining the birds being too scared to fly. "I wonder where the witch *is*?" she remarked, gazing around the empty, cloudless sky. "She must be able to fly very fast if we can't even see her."

Just as Summer was saying these words, Ellie gasped and pointed downwards. A

dark shape had emerged from the trees
and was shooting towards them, hunched
low over her broomstick. "There she is!"
Ellie cried.

"Your Majesty, prepare for attack!"
called Swoop anxiously as the witch sped
faster through the sky. "Here she comes!"

The Wicked Witch was flying incredibly fast, Summer realised, shrinking lower on Swoop's back in fright. She had a pale green face, long straggly hair and the coldest, meanest eyes Summer had ever seen. Just like the illustration in her book of fairytales!

The witch let out another horrible high-pitched cackle. "Oh, goody! Target practice!" she screeched, her voice carrying on the wind. "I spy with my little eye, trespassers flying in my sky! Let's see…who shall I aim for first?" She screamed with laughter as she caught sight of King Merry on the Swan Queen's back. "A king and a queen together – that's perfect. Two for the price of one!"

She held out her index finger and

purple streaks of magic crackled and sparked from its tip, making her surge forward even faster on her broomstick.

The Swan Queen had to dive sharply to her left to avoid the witch crashing into her. "Please return to the ground," she ordered the witch. "You are flying too dangerously and breaking our Sky Rules."

"Ha!" screeched the witch, swerving to follow the queen. "Who cares? Rules are meant to be broken, that's what I say. And so are foolish birds! Ha!"

"Help!" wailed King Merry, hanging on for dear life as the queen dodged away again. "I feel sick!"

"Hold on, Your Highness!" Trixi called anxiously from where she was still tucked in Ellie's pocket. "Just hold tight!"

The witch turned neatly in mid-air, purple magic flickering and flashing around her. "We'll see how *merry* you are after a crash landing, dear king!" she crowed as she shot directly for the queen again.

Ellie hardly dared look as the Swan Queen twisted, swooped and dived to avoid the witch. King Merry clutched at his crown as it slipped on his head and almost fell off the Swan Queen's back. "We've got to do something," Ellie called to her friends in fright. "We've got to stop her!"

"I know!" Summer yelled back. "We need to help the Swan Queen. But how?"

The Dreadful Duo

Jasmine thought hard. "Longfeather, can we distract the witch?" she asked her swan. "Maybe if we all start weaving about in front of her, she won't know who to chase. That way the queen can escape."

"Good thinking, Jasmine," said Trixi.

"That's an excellent idea," Longfeather agreed. "Swoop, Silver, did you hear? Let's protect our queen!"

The three swans surged into action.
Ellie could hardly bear to keep her eyes
open as they all dived in front of the
Swan Queen, twisting, twirling and
looping. She was sure they would crash
into one another – or into the queen
herself – but amazingly the swans seemed
to time their moves perfectly. Not a
single feather was touched!

Jasmine thought this was the most exciting thing ever. It was better than any roller coaster, riding on Longfeather's back as he soared and spun. Best of all, their plan seemed to be working. The witch looked very confused! She hovered on her broomstick, blinking at the whirling white birds, trying to pick out which was the queen.

"Hey! That's cheating!" she shouted, scowling. "Stop that!"

The brave swans took no notice and carried on flying in wild patterns all around her. The witch, meanwhile, was stuck in the middle. Every time she tried to fly away, one of the swans would swoop in front of her to stop her going any further. She was trapped!

Ellie noticed with a thankful smile that

the Swan Queen had seized the chance to slip away, flying herself and King Merry back to the safety of the palace. Already she was just a white speck far off in the distance.

The witch let out a scream of frustration. "Stupid swans! This is *my* sky now and if you don't get out of the way, I'll turn you into pigeons. What do you think of that, eh?"

The girls heard the witch chanting what sounded like a magic spell under her breath.

"I think we should go," Jasmine said urgently. She didn't want the horrid witch to cast any spells on the brave swans.

"I agree. The queen will be back at the palace by now," said Swoop. "Let's have one last turn around the witch and return there too."

The three swans whizzed around the witch at top speed, sending her broomstick into a spin. "Heeeelp!" she shrieked as she clung to the handle.

"Quick – let's go," said Silver, flapping her wings hard. "Before she gets her breath back and comes after us."

The three swans soared through the sky, back over the forest and across the lake. Then they swooped down into the palace courtyard and landed gracefully.

Ellie, Summer and Jasmine clambered off the swans' backs, their legs shaky. "Phew!" said Jasmine. "Thank you, Longfeather."

"My pleasure," he replied, transforming back into a swan-person. His eyes twinkled. "Any time."

Swoop and Silver transformed too, and approached the Swan Queen who was sitting on her throne. She was also in her human form, and looked very unhappy. "I don't know what the witch

wants with me," the queen said sadly,
"but I can't put the rest of you in danger
again."

"You mustn't
blame yourself,"
the king
exclaimed, his
red cheeks
puffing out.
"That witch
is worse
than my
sister."

But the queen was already removing
the crown. "It's my job as the guardian
of the skies to protect all birds," she said.
"And if I can't even protect my own
swans...I shouldn't have the sky crown
any more."

Ellie blinked, suddenly remembering what the witch had said earlier. "*This is my sky now,*" she had cackled. *Was that what she was doing here,* Ellie wondered *– trying to take control of the sky instead of the Swan Queen?*

"Your Majesty," she blurted out. "I think the witch wants your crown. I think *she* wants to rule the skies. We mustn't let her!"

"No way," Jasmine agreed.

"Absolutely not," King Merry said. "The sky crown is yours, Your Majesty. You are the royally appointed guardian, and that's the way it shall stay."

The little king folded his arms and sat down with nod. But a bloodcurdling cackle greeted his words. "Not if I've got anything to do with it," called the witch, circling above their heads, her eyes glinting colder than ever. "Now…where are my dear little helpers?"

The witch clicked her fingers and the sky darkened as three thunderclouds rolled in. The girls stared in horror as they recognised the creatures riding on the thunderclouds.

"Storm Sprites!" gulped Summer.

The Storm Sprites were Queen Malice's henchmen, and were every bit as nasty as their wicked leader. They had large, black, bat-like wings and cold, ugly faces with spiky hair.

The Swan Queen stood up.
"I command you all to leave this palace immediately," she told the Storm Sprites. "You are not welcome."

"You heard her," the king added, making shooing motions with his arms. "Go on, this minute!"

The witch merely tipped back her head and gave another scream of laughter. The Storm Sprites jeered and flicked fat, glistening raindrops from their fingertips, showering the swans below.

"Misery drops!" Jasmine shouted as she recognised the watery missiles. "Duck!"

The girls dodged out of the way and most of the drops spattered down without hitting anybody, but some of the swan-people were taken by surprise. *Splash! Splatter!* went the misery drops as they fell on the swan-people. Each time one was hit, a mini raincloud appeared above their head, soaking them with water. Misery drops usually made the people they hit too sad to move, but to the girls' surprise, the soaking swans just laughed.

"Is that the best you can do?" Longfeather chuckled as a cloud started to rain on him. "Don't you know we swans love water?"

"A nice cool shower is just what I needed," another swan-person shouted bravely. "Thank you very much!"

The Storm Sprites scowled and muttered to each other.

"I think they're going to give up!" Ellie said hopefully. But then she spotted an even bigger thundercloud on the horizon. "Uh-oh," she gulped, nudging her friends. "Maybe not. Look!"

This thundercloud was very long and very dark. It swept across the lake like a huge black carpet unrolling.

"Oh, goody, my new friend is here," cackled the witch gleefully as a tall, thin woman appeared on the thundercloud. She wore a spiky crown and a long black cloak, and below her frizzy black hair the girls could see her sneering face.

King Merry turned pale. "Malice!" he cried. "What are you doing here?"

Summer, Jasmine and Ellie huddled

together. "This just got a whole lot worse," Jasmine hissed to her friends. "The Wicked Witch and Queen Malice are working together!"

An Evil Argument

The thundercloud completely blotted out the sun. Then it started sinking lower and lower, rolling like dark smoke into the palace courtyard.

"Quick, Trixi!" Summer gasped, thinking fast. "Can you use your magic to send the Swan Queen somewhere safe? There's no other way for her to escape!"

Trixi nodded, her blue eyes wide and anxious. Quickly she tapped her pixie ring, just as Queen Malice and the Wicked Witch landed in the courtyard together.

"Make the Swan Queen disappear,
And—"

Trixi began, but Queen Malice fixed her with a steely glare.

"Silence!" she boomed, thudding her black thunderbolt staff down on the stone floor. Black magic crackled from its tip and the shimmering pink light which had begun shining from Trixi's pixie ring immediately vanished, like a candle being blown out.

The swan-people gathered together in

front of their queen,
standing between
her and the
witch.

"Move
aside,
birdies,"
sneered the
Wicked
Witch. "We
want a word
with your queen."

"Never!" cried Silver defiantly, her chin
high as she and the other swan-people
linked arms, forming a chain.

Jasmine gasped as she watched the
courageous swans. But to her surprise,
the Swan Queen gently broke through
the crowd.

"No," she said. "I cannot allow this.
You must not risk your safety for me."

"Your Majesty — no!" cried Swoop and
some other swans in alarm, but the Swan
Queen bravely stepped forward and
stood in front of the Wicked Witch and
Queen Malice.

"Why are you here?" she asked calmly. "Why are you disturbing the peace of our skies?"

Queen Malice gave the most horrible smirk. "We're here for your crown," she replied, pointing a finger at it. "And that's what we shall have!"

Magic crackled from Queen Malice's finger, like wisps of black smoke. The smoky magic rushed towards the silver crown and pulled it out of the Swan Queen's hands, sending it floating over the courtyard towards Queen Malice.

The witch let out a triumphant cry. "Give it to me, Malice, my dear," she crooned. "I shall rule the skies, while you rule the land!"

Jasmine noticed a strange expression on Malice's face. Was Queen Malice really going to share her power with the Wicked Witch? She turned to King Merry in surprise. "I didn't think your sister would be good at sharing," she whispered.

King Merry spluttered. "She's never been able to share anything, not even her toys when we were children," he whispered in reply.

"In that case…" Jasmine thought for a moment, then smiled. "Maybe we can stir up a bit of trouble between Malice and the witch."

"What do you mean?" Ellie asked.

"How?" Summer wondered.

Jasmine grinned. "Watch this," she replied. Then she raised her voice and addressed the witch. "Wait a minute," she said. "You're going to rule the kingdom together?"

The witch scowled. "Haven't you been listening to a word I've said?" she snapped. "Yes, that's exactly what we're going to do!"

Jasmine laughed as if this was the funniest thing she'd ever heard. Ellie and Summer stared at their friend, not sure what she was up to.

The witch stared too. "What?" she shrieked. "What's so amusing?"

Jasmine wiped her eyes, still grinning broadly. "And you actually believe that, do you?" she asked the witch. "Oh dear. Because I think Queen Malice is secretly planning to keep the sky crown for herself!"

Queen Malice whirled round with such a furious scowl that Jasmine was sure she had guessed correctly.

The Wicked Witch looked startled for a moment, then shook her head. "Don't be ridiculous, child," she snapped. "Queen Malice and I will rule together! Tell them, Malice!"

Ellie and Summer hid their smiles as Queen Malice scowled. Now they understood exactly what Jasmine was trying to do – make them argue! The sky crown hovered between the two evil women as if it wasn't sure where to go.

"You really shouldn't believe everything Malice tells you," Ellie warned the witch. "Don't trust her!"

"Yeah," Summer added. "Queen Malice will never let *you* be guardian of the skies. No way!"

"The sky crown is mine!" the witch

stormed, grabbing the crown out of the
air and attempting to push it down over
her black hat. "So there!"

"Silence!" Queen Malice snapped.
"I should be the one ruling the *whole*
kingdom, rather than my stupid brother.
First I'll rule the skies, then the rest of the
kingdom!"

"What?" the witch replied, shaking her fists. "But you promised *I'd* rule the skies! You can't cheat a witch. I won't let you!"

The girls stepped back as a ferocious argument began. Queen Malice snapped her fingers and a whirl of black smoke knocked the silver crown from the witch's head. Then she muttered a string of magic words that sent the crown whizzing through the air towards her.

Bristling with fury, the Wicked Witch promptly chanted a spell that sent the crown flying back to *her*. Soon the courtyard was crackling with magic and thunderbolts.

"Quick," Ellie hissed to Trixi. "While they're busy arguing, let's open the fairytale book!"

Trixi pulled the tiny fairytale book from her pocket and tapped her pixie ring. Instantly, the book grew larger and floated into Summer's hands. She flicked through it until she reached a page with a picture of the Wicked Witch on it.

"There!" she cried, opening the book wide.

At once, the picture glowed silver and purple and long lines of light shot out from it, flying all the way over to the witch.

"No!" she screeched as the glittering light took hold of her and began dragging her across the courtyard.

"It's sucking her back into the book!" Jasmine cheered.

The witch thrashed around wildly, digging her heels into the ground as the light pulled her towards the fairytale book. She scrambled out of the light, and the girls gasped.

But then Queen Malice leaned forwards, and with one big push she shoved the Wicked Witch towards the book. The light wrapped round the witch tightly, dragging her towards the fluttering pages.

"It's mine!" howled the witch, reaching out a hand and grabbing the crown. "You promised!"

Queen Malice lunged towards the witch and snatched hold of the other side of the crown. The light around the witch grew brighter and brighter, but neither of them let go. The light twisted up the Wicked Witch's arm and wrapped round the crown. All of a sudden there was a horrible cracking sound – and the crown snapped in two!

"Noooooo!" screamed the witch, her voice growing fainter and fainter as she vanished into the book, leaving only the faint smell of smoke behind her.

Jasmine cheered and Ellie jumped up and down in delight. But Summer couldn't stop staring at the pieces of the Swan Queen's crown lying on the floor. The sky crown was broken!

The Guardian
of the Skies

"Oh, no!" Ellie gasped as she spotted the broken crown. "Maybe we can fix it—" she started to say, but her voice trailed away as Queen Malice gave a furious screech.

Her frizzy hair standing on end, Malice stamped on the silver pieces until they were little more than rubble and dust.

"If I can't have the sky crown, nobody will!" she spat.

Lightning crackled in the sky above them, flashing cold silver light, and thunder rumbled round the courtyard. Gesturing to the Storm Sprites, Queen Malice swooped away on her thundercloud in an almighty huff. The Sprites' bat-like wings rustled and then they were gone too.

The courtyard was silent for a moment. "Well!" King Merry exclaimed with a sigh, pushing his spectacles back up his nose. "I must say, that sister of mine gets worse every day. I do apologise for her terrible behaviour."

Ellie dropped to her knees and began gathering up the largest parts of the broken crown. The silver was tarnished and dusty, and even though Ellie was good at making things, she knew that mending the crown would be very difficult.

Jasmine and Summer helped her. "This is going to be the hardest jigsaw ever," Summer said, feeling upset.

"But we've got to try," Jasmine added. She took a deep breath and raised her eyes to the Swan Queen. "It was a really bad idea, getting the Wicked Witch and Queen Malice to fight over your crown," she said meekly. "I'm so sorry it got broken."

To the girls' surprise, the Swan Queen didn't look angry, or even very upset. "Don't worry," she said kindly. "It doesn't matter."

But this only made Jasmine feel worse. Of course it mattered that the crown was broken! She hung her head, hot colour staining her cheeks.

"Thank you for everything you did," the Swan Queen said simply. "You were very brave. Now that the witch is back in the fairytale book, our skies will be safe once more."

"But your crown..." Summer faltered.

The Swan Queen smiled and pressed her hands together before touching them gently to her forehead. Silver and gold sparkles swirled around her as she transformed back into a swan. Then she gracefully moved her long neck so the girls could see the tuft of white feathers still on top of her head. The tuft was circular, Jasmine noticed, with the feathers all pointing upwards. Just like the points of a crown!

King Merry's eyes twinkled. "This is the *real* sky crown that belongs to the guardian of the skies," he explained. "So, you see, nobody can steal it, nor take the guardian's powers." He laughed. "And if the Wicked Witch and my wretched sister knew anything about being a sky-guardian, they'd have known that!"

Jasmine gave the most enormous sigh of relief. "I'm really glad to hear that," she said. "A crown of feathers suits you perfectly, Your Majesty!"

"Thank you," said the Swan Queen, her eyes twinkling. "And now, my swans, we have work to do. We must spread the word to all our bird friends that the skies are safe once more." She cocked her head to one side thoughtfully as she turned back to the girls. "You are welcome to join us, my dears, if you'd like to help."

Summer's eyes lit up. Go soaring through the air again to pass on the good news? See all kinds of magical birds flying freely through the Secret Kingdom? Of *course* she wanted to help! "Yes, please!" she said without hesitating.

"That would be great," Jasmine agreed happily, clapping her hands together.

Even Ellie wanted to help share the
great news. "That makes three of us,"
she said with a grin. "Thank you!"

King Merry beamed. "Marvellous,"
he declared. "Splendid! Now, if you'll
excuse me, I'm going to return to the
Enchanted Palace to
work on a new
invention."
He tapped
his nose
mysteriously.
"I think this
might be my
best one yet!"

Trixi smiled.
"I'm sure it will be, Your
Highness," she said encouragingly. She
tapped her pixie ring and a sparkly light

surrounded the little king, who waved
as he faded away. After King Merry
disappeared, the Swan Queen shook
out her wings and stretched them wide.
"Let's take to the skies!" she cried.

ᘒSafe Skiesᕬ

With a shimmer of magic and a rustle
of feathers, the swan-people transformed
into swans once more and prepared to
take off. Swoop, Silver and Longfeather
all made their way across to the girls and
dipped their heads to them.

"May we carry you again?"
Longfeather asked politely.

"Yes, please," Jasmine said, climbing onto his soft back.

"Thanks, Swoop," Summer said, taking care not to ruffle his snow-white feathers as she clambered on. "I will enjoy this even more now I know the witch isn't trying to hurt anyone."

Silver gave Ellie a friendly wink. "Hop on," she said. "We can fly as low or high as you want this time. And I'll take you to see the magical laughter birds. They are so sweet!"

Ellie grinned. She liked the sound of that! "Thank you," she replied, grateful for Silver's kindness. "Ready when you are!"

One by one, the swans took off into the air. Trixi flew with Ellie once more as she and Silver soared upwards, closely followed by Longfeather and Swoop carrying Jasmine and Summer. The Swan Queen led the flock, singing out a lilting song as they flew over the forest.

"Skies are clear, skies are clear,
There's no need for you to fear.
You're free to fly, the sky is ours,
I'll keep you safe with all my powers."

The words and melody sent a shiver down Summer's spine, and then she cried out in excitement as she saw a huge flock of birds appearing from the trees below. "Ellie, Jasmine, look!" she called.

It really was a beautiful sight. Birds of every colour and size were filling the sky – from mighty eagles with keen eyes and hooked beaks, right down to a group of tiny purple birds, their wings flecked with gleaming silver feathers. Out flew sleepy brown owls that hooted for joy once they

realised the witch had gone. Out flew the
pure white peace doves, two at a time,
cooing happily to one another.

"Even the insects are celebrating,"
Jasmine noticed, pointing to where
shimmering dragonflies danced happily,
and tiny spotty ladybirds flew dizzily
together, looping the loop and chasing
after one another.

"Where are the laughter birds?" Ellie asked Silver, eagerly scanning the skies.

"They'll be in the flower meadow," Silver replied. "Nearly there!"

She swooped lower as the forest gave way to rolling grassy meadows filled with flowers. Ellie could see scarlet poppies and tall white daisies as well as all sorts of flowers she didn't recognise – pretty pink bell-shaped ones that jingled in the

breeze, masses of yellow flowers shaped
like moons and stars, and a clump of
lilac blooms with lacy petals, which
smelled absolutely delicious.

"It's gorgeous," Ellie sighed, beaming
and waving at Summer and Jasmine,
whose swans were also gliding low over
the meadow.

At the far end of the meadow was a
tall tree, with golden pears gleaming
amidst its leafy branches.

"Laughter birds! Laughter birds! You're
safe to come out," called Silver as she
flew near the tree. "The Wicked Witch
has gone, the skies are safe."

For a moment, Ellie, Jasmine and
Summer thought nothing was going
to happen. But then they heard a
sweet little giggle, and a feathered face

peeped out shyly
from between
the leaves –
followed by
another, and
another.
And
then the
whole tree
seemed to
be shaking
with little
laughing blue
birds – it was such
an infectious sound, you
couldn't help joining in!

"Come out, there's no need to be shy," Swoop called.

Still giggling, five pretty birds sailed out

of the pear tree and
flew towards
the girls. They
had feathers
of bright
blue, and tiny
golden beaks
and feet. Ellie
smiled in delight. With
their cheeky giggles, they really were the
most adorable birds she'd ever seen!

The birds fluttered around the meadow,
singing and giggling together. Ellie,
Jasmine and Summer felt really proud
that they had helped make the skies safe
again.

"I'll never forget this," Summer said
dreamily. "I'm so glad the birds can fly
freely again. Don't they look happy?"

"They do," beamed Trixi. "And it's all thanks to you three – and the swans. But now, I'm afraid it's time to—"

"Nooooo!" cried Jasmine before the little pixie could finish her sentence. "Don't send us back yet, Trixi, please! We're having such fun here."

Trixi smiled. "I'm sorry," she said. "But it really is time you were back in your own world. Besides," she added, pulling a funny face, "I dread to think what King Merry is getting up to without me!"

Longfeather, Swoop and Silver flew gently to the ground and the girls clambered off their backs. "Thank you," Ellie said, hugging her swan.

"Thank *you*," replied the swans as Jasmine and Summer said the same.

"You are welcome at Swan Palace

any time," said the Swan Queen herself,
landing beside them. "And you are true
friends of the swans, now and for ever
more."

Trixi flew up and kissed each girl on
the nose. "I'm sure we'll see you soon,"
she said, then tapped her pixie ring.
"Goodbye for now!"

Her ring glowed and then a sparkling whirlwind appeared, lifting up the girls and whisking them away from the Secret Kingdom. Jasmine, Summer and Ellie just had time to call out their last goodbyes before they felt themselves landing back in Summer's bedroom, where the film was still playing. It was as if they had never been away.

"Wow," Ellie said with a big grin. "That was amazing."

Jasmine bounced happily on Summer's bed. "So now the Wicked Witch is back in the fairytale book along with the giant, that means there are only four more baddies to find."

Summer nodded happily. "But now," she said, walking over to the TV, "let's finish watching this film, shall we?"

Ellie and Jasmine both looked at her in surprise. "I thought you said it was too scary earlier?" Ellie asked.

Summer grinned sheepishly. "I know," she said, "but that was before I came face to face with a real wicked witch!" She laughed and sat down on the bed. "How could I possibly be scared of someone on TV after that?"

"Yay, Summer!" Jasmine cheered.

Ellie laughed too, and squeezed in between her two best friends. "Anyway," she said, "I reckon this film will have a happy ending. All the best adventures have one of those, right?"

"Right!" her friends chorused. The three girls sat and watched the film together, all looking forward to *their* next adventure. *It might be a scary one,* thought Summer with a little shiver. *It might be an exciting one,* thought Jasmine hopefully.

But one thing was for sure, thought Ellie. *Any adventure in the Secret Kingdom was definitely going to be a magical one!*

**In the next Secret Kingdom
adventure, Ellie, Summer and
Jasmine visit**

Snow Bear Sanctuary

Read on for a sneak peek...

At the Zoo

The leopard cub pounced on a fallen leaf
and rolled onto its back. "Oh, isn't he
cute!" Summer Hammond squealed as
the cub wrestled with the leaf and then
yowled at the people watching from
outside his enclosure at Honeyvale Zoo.
"I wish I could cuddle him," Summer
said longingly as she turned to her two

best friends, Ellie Macdonald and Jasmine Smith.

"Just like you wanted to cuddle the wombat we saw, and the chipmunks and the baby elephant," laughed Jasmine.

"I think you'd even cuddle a stick insect if you could, Summer!" teased Ellie.

Summer grinned. "Yep, but the leopard cub is definitely my favourite." She looked to where the cub was now wobbling his way along a branch. "I'm so glad your mum and grandma decided to bring us to the zoo today, Jasmine."

"Me too." Ellie grinned. It was a bright, crisp autumn day, perfect for visiting the zoo! "There are so many amazing animals and birds here. I like the parrots best," she added, thinking of the brightly coloured birds they'd seen swooping round a big aviary earlier. "They were such beautiful colours. I'd love to paint them."

"I like the orang-utans," said Jasmine. She jumped up and down, her dark ponytail bouncing on her shoulders. "OO-OO-OO! I'd like to be like a orang-utan and make lots of noise!"

"You already do!" grinned Ellie.

Jasmine giggled.

"Where should we go next?" Summer asked.

"There's a map over there," Jasmine pointed out. They all ran over to a big board showing a map of the whole zoo. It was covered with colourful pictures of the elephant, zebra and giraffe enclosures, the penguin pool, the monkey cages and the houses where the snakes and bats and insects lived.

"This reminds me of another map," Jasmine said. She dropped her voice to a whisper. "The map of the Secret Kingdom!"

The girls exchanged smiles. They shared an amazing secret. Ever since they'd found a magical box at their school jumble sale, they'd been on lots of amazing adventures in an enchanted land called the Secret Kingdom.

"I wonder when we'll get another message from the Secret Kingdom?" said Summer.

"I bet it won't be long," replied Jasmine. "Not with four fairytale baddies still on the loose!"

Evil Queen Malice was always trying

to cause problems in the kingdom because she wanted to rule instead of her brother, the kindly King Merry. Her latest wicked plan had been to release six baddies from a book of fairytales into the kingdom. She hoped that they would cause so much trouble that the people would beg her to rule just to make them stop. So far the girls had managed to put a giant and a wicked witch back into the book but there were still four more scary fairytale characters to find.

"I wonder who we'll have to stop next," said Ellie.

"And how fierce they'll be," added Summer, playing nervously with the end of one of her long blonde pigtails. The giant and witch had both been horrible!

"We'd better be ready to go at any

time," said Jasmine. "Maybe we should check the box. It might have a message for us."

Summer took her bag off her back. She had brought the box with her just in case their friends in the Secret Kingdom tried to send them a message. But just as she started to open the top of her bag, she heard Mrs Smith, Jasmine's mum, calling to them.

"Yoo-hoo, girls! Over here!" Jasmine's mum was coming out of the nearby café where she had been having a cup of tea with Jasmine's grandma.

"We'll look at the box later," Jasmine whispered.

"Shall we go and see the penguins now?" suggested Mrs Smith.

The girls nodded eagerly. They all

loved the penguins with their funny waddling walk and their twinkly black eyes. They set off with Jasmine's mum and grandma. As they neared the penguin pool, Summer hung back a little. She wanted to check the Magic Box just in case there was a message from their friends.

She opened the top of her bag excitedly, just in time to see a spark of light flash across the mirror, followed by another and another. Suddenly the whole box glowed with a bright light!

Summer gave a squeak of surprise and hastily shut the bag so no one could see. She had to tell the others!

She rushed over to where Jasmine and Ellie were staring down into the penguin pool. Mrs Smith was looking at the information board to see what time the penguins were being fed and Jasmine's grandma was chatting to another family who were also watching the penguins.

"Jasmine! Ellie!" Summer whispered. "The Magic Box is glowing!"

"Oh, wow!" Ellie hissed. "Is there a message?"

"I didn't see. I couldn't look for long."

Jasmine glanced round. "Let's go over there where it's quiet."

She led the way over to another sign. It was big enough for them to stand behind without being seen. The girls ducked behind it and Summer opened her bag again. Sparkling light spilled out. Excitement rushed through the girls as they saw words forming in the mirrored lid. It was the riddle that would whisk

them away! They were having a great
time at the zoo, but going to the Secret
Kingdom would be even better!

Snow Bear Sanctuary

to find out what
happens next!

Secret Kingdom

Series 3

When Queen Malice releases six fairytale baddies into the Secret Kingdom, it's up to the girls to find them!

Secret Kingdom

Be in on the secret.
Collect them all!

Series 1

When Jasmine, Summer and Ellie discover
the magical land of the Secret Kingdom,
a whole world of adventure awaits!

Secret Kingdom

Have you read all the books in

Bubble
Volcano

ROSIE BANKS

Sugarsweet
Bakery

ROSIE BANKS

Dream Dale

ROSIE BANKS

Lily Pad
Lake

ROSIE BANKS

Midnight
Maze

ROSIE BANKS

Fairytale
Forest

ROSIE BANKS

Series 2

Wicked Queen Malice has cast a spell to
turn King Merry into a toad! Can the girls
find six magic ingredients to save him?

Secret Kingdom

Have you read all the books in Series Four?

Meet the magical Animal Keepers of the Secret Kingdom, who spread fun, friendship, kindness and bravery throughout the land!

In **Magic Seal**, Ellie, Summer and Jasmine must reunite the Seal Keeper with his magical charm to make the Secret Kingdom fun again!

Can you find a way through the maze to reach the seal? Watch out for Storm Sprites!